For My Love

LIFE

Many thought she was strong and resilient

Little did they know she was scared

But not scared of what could happen

Rather, scared of what she was capable of

If pushed past her limits

Tired. Exhausted. Drained.

Some days are worse than others

There is no end to the things

That require her energy

She wants it to stop

She needs it to end

If these things keep

Taking her energy

There won't be any left for her

She sometimes sensationalizes the end

Her end

Her final days

And surprisingly it doesn't scare her

In the least

Is that wrong?

How much can a person endure?

How much will be enough to break me?

I've been close

So very close to the edge

Luckily, there are some

Who have pulled me back

Without them,

I wouldn't be here still

The other side of the pendulum is the narcissist

No one comes close to the standards they set

They are incapable of loving another

No child, no spouse, or family member compares

Anger bubbles beneath the surface

It's always there even on the good days

She wishes it away and yet it returns

Day after day

No matter how hard she tries

Anger is her mask for something

But for what exactly?

Her eyes are dull

They have been that way for years

Not a day goes by that he wishes

She would have that spark again

What can be done

To bring the light back to her eyes?

Is it even possible anymore

Or has it gone on far too long

To return to the natural state

Of inner joy?

If you look deep enough into her eyes

You can see the past hurt

The trauma she has endured

The obstacles she has faced

If you look deep enough into her soul

You can feel the pain inside

The low self-worth

The anxiety just below the surface

If you cared enough to go beyond

The walls she's erected

You may just see who she really is inside

And learn how to love her

How fair is it that she has it all?

The husband, the kids, the job, the life

Always so put together and proper

Until one day I realize it's a façade

Cracks in the exterior show the core

Husbands cheat, kids have problems

Jobs can be office prisons

And the life is fake

I prefer my real world

Some days she wishes it would all end
The pain, the hurt, the exhaustion
She is tired of explaining
Tired of being responsible
Overwhelmed with grief and
Sadness that only she can feel

How is it that no one can see this
Or understand her position?
Some days she thinks she is going crazy
And other days she thinks
The world is crazy, and she is sane

LOVE

I've loved you long before you reciprocated

I took a chance and pined away for you

Waiting

It worked in my favor

One day you realized you loved me too

My dreams came true

But not without some nightmares in between

Each morning I roll over and count my blessings

You are still here through thick and thin

Just like you promised all those years ago

It took a lot of work to get over that wall I built

But I let you inside

I still occasionally hope it wasn't a mistake

My secrets haunt me

Hold my hand my love
A simple act but one that means
So very much to me

Hold my hand my dear
I need your touch and presence with me

Hold my hand my darling
Keep me balanced and grounded
As I waver

Hold my hand my love
You hold my heart

I cherish our morning walks

The quiet conversation as we stroll

The warmth of the sun on our faces

As you feed my soul

Some women boast

With their jewelry and extravagant vacations

While I revel in this stillness that is us

Their lavish gifts are far between

But my love gives me these times often

And honestly, it works better in my favor

Where do you fall?

You should love others as you love yourself

Draw that line to love others

But be mindful of your own needs

Find the balance

I wish I could take away the pain for you

The torment, the uncertainty

Of all the things I can do

This is one that is beyond my abilities

So instead, I will sit with you

Comfort you and offer my attention

As you speak those words

That neither of us want to hear

But now we have to

Face this demon head on

And make plans for

The unforeseeable future

One that we did not choose

LOSS

Your hands are soft

From the many hours of use

Your eyes are tired

Having seen so much

Your arms are weak

From the years of embraces

Your breath is slower

Without an urgency

But

You are content

The time has come

So many of your days were filled with love

Your life has been full

You are grateful for every day you were gifted

It never gets easier

Saying goodbye to a loved one

Is hard anytime

I will hold tight to my memories of you

Until we meet again

Sorrowful brown eyes begging for help

A small whimper escapes his throat

I gently stroke his head and speak softly

My boy is suffering and it's time

I have loved you for your entire life

You have been my best companion

No other one can replace you

Such a good boy

Her hands sink deep into the earth

The warmth soothes her soul

The deep smell penetrates her nose

Tending to her garden, she relaxes

There is no rush to finish this

Just time to enjoy the quietness

The stillness

Briefly, she looks up and sees

The figure watching her

In a flash, he is gone

She is left with an overwhelming

Sense of love and comfort

Her Grandfather visits her often

As I move through my life

I can sense you

In everything I see

In everything around me

Your laugh in the gentle breeze

The color of your hair in the leaves

The skies in the morning were your favorite

The warmth of your soul from the sun

Even though I can no longer see you

I can feel you in the world around me

You showed me love

By being there for me

For holding my hand

And listening to my worries

You showed me love

By helping to guide me

In my stressful times

And seeing me through

You showed me love

By loving our children

And providing for us

With all that you do

You showed me love

And eventually how to love myself

Is it possible to love someone

More than yourself?

The answer will depend

On how much you love yourself

There are some who have

A depleted sense of self-worth

For them, loving others is easy

Their children, their spouse, their friends

Everyone else comes before them

The sunlight reflects off the ice crystals

On the cold winter morning

The air is crisp and fresh

My boots crush the stiff ground as I walk

The color of the morning sky reminds me of you

How the amber resembles your hair

And the quiet calm mirrors your personality

You are no longer walking this earth

But I can still feel you

In everything around me

Watching and encouraging me

At every step

You gave me the chance to see things differently

From your own perspective

I was unable to see what you can

But you are showing me a kaleidoscope

That I never knew was there

I will be forever grateful to you

For believing in me

And showing me how positive life can be

Even on those dark days

When my mind wants to tell me otherwise

He has your eyes

Your lopsided smile

And your love of the outdoors

He has my dark curls

Those clumsy feet we share

And a desire to please those we love

He loves watching the birds on our walks

He talks to you often in the warm breeze

He prays to God that you are better now

We both miss you so much

Your place at the table sits empty

You fill our hearts now with memories

Those days are now gone

And we move on without you

We miss you my love

I open my eyes and for a split second

I forget

I roll over to see your face, kiss your lips,

Embrace you

But you are no longer here

As I come back to consciousness

I remember

You are gone from this earth

From my life

All that remains are the photos and memories

That I hold dear to my heart

How will I exist without your presence

Today I decide not to

Slip back into my dreams

Of a time when we had each other

I will learn to deal with your absence later

I revel in my memories and dreams of you

And enjoy the time we had

If only in my dreams

Grief and loss are inevitable

As you grow older

But they happen far too often

Early in life

Losing loved ones is never easy

When they are taken from us too soon

Feelings of anger and resentment surface

It's so hard not to place blame

For the life that has been shortened

It's in God's plan they say

It's not for us to judge

Or understand they say

But that doesn't make it any easier

No one can ever replace you

There is a place in my heart that remains

Dedicated to you and everything we had together

Losing you was so tragic

It took me years to climb

Out of my abyss

He has found me and saved me from myself

You would like him

He has shown me life and love

Even after all this

That I can still move forward

And love again

I'm allowed to be happy and thrive

Even after you have gone

You have given me so many gifts

The gift of love

From you and permission for me to love myself

Even after all I've been through and done

The gift of feeling

Your expressions and the allowance

Of my feelings unhinged

The gift of patience

As I learn how to heal and grow

Evolving to a better future

The gift of understanding

As you struggle to interpret my position

And move forward with my life